JAMES

PERCY

THERE ARE 36 EXCITING THOMAS TITLES
TO COLLECT IN THE BUZZ BOOK SERIES

Look out for all our other books
about Thomas and his friends
available from Heinemann,
Mammoth and Dean

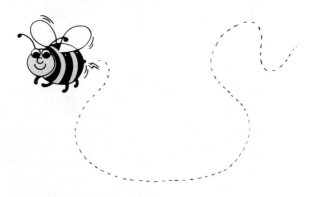

First published in Great Britain 1990 by Buzz Books
an imprint of Reed Children's Books
Michelin House, 81 Fulham Road, London SW3 6RB
and Auckland, Melbourne, Singapore and Toronto
Reprinted 1993 (three times) and 1994 (twice)

Copyright © William Heinemann Limited 1990
All publishing rights: William Heinemann Ltd
All television and merchandising rights
licensed by William Heinemann Limited to
Britt Allcroft (Thomas) Limited, exclusively, worldwide.

Photographs © Britt Allcroft (Thomas) Ltd 1985, 1986
Photographs by David Mitton, Kenny McArthur and
Terry Permane for Britt Allcroft's production of
Thomas the Tank Engine and Friends

ISBN 1 85591 002 0

Printed and bound in Italy by Olivotto

PERCY RUNS AWAY

buzz books

When Thomas the Tank Engine was given his own branch line there was only Edward who would do the shunting for the big engines.

Edward liked shunting and playing with trucks, but the others would not help him. They said that shunting was not a job for

important Tender Engines, it was a job for common Tank Engines.

The Fat Controller was very cross. He kept them in the shed and said that they could only come out when they stopped being naughty. Then he sent for Thomas to come and help Edward to run the line for a few days.

Henry, James and Gordon were in the shed for several days. They were very miserable and longed to be let out.

At last, the Fat Controller arrived.

"I hope that you are sorry," he said sternly, "and understand that you are not so important after all." He told them that he had a surprise for them!

"We have a new Tank Engine called Percy. He is a smart little green engine, with four wheels. Percy has helped to pull the coaches and Thomas and Edward have worked the main line very nicely, while you have been away."

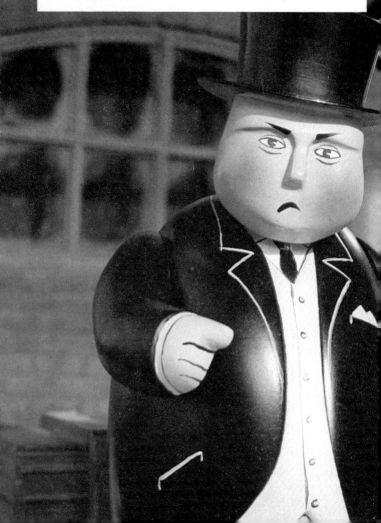

"But I will let you out now if you promise to be good," he said.

"Yes, sir," said the three engines.

"We will."

"That's right," said the Fat Controller. "But please remember that this 'no shunting' nonsense must stop."

The Fat Controller told Thomas, Edward and Percy that they could go and play on the branch line for a few days. They ran off happily to find Annie and Clarabel at the junction.

Annie and Clarabel were Thomas's two coaches and they were very pleased to see Thomas back again. Edward and Percy played with the trucks.

"Stop! Stop! Stop!" screamed the trucks as they were pushed into their proper sidings. But the two engines laughed and went on shunting until the trucks were in their right places.

Next, Edward took some trucks to the Quarry.

Percy was left alone, but he didn't mind a bit. He liked watching the trains and being cheeky to the other engines.

"Hurry, hurry, hurry," he would call and they got very cross.

After a great deal of shunting on
Thomas's branch line, Percy was waiting for
the signalman to set the points so that he
could get back to the yard. He was eager to
work, but he was being rather careless and
was not paying attention.

16

Edward had told Percy about the signals on the main line.

"Be careful on that main line," he warned. "Whistle to the signalman to let him know that you are there."

But Percy forgot all about Edward's warning.

He didn't remember to whistle and the signalman forgot he was there.

Percy waited and waited.

The points were still against him so he couldn't move. Then he looked along the main line.

"Peep! Peep!" he whistled in horror.

"Peep! peep!" he whistled again, for rushing straight towards him was Gordon with the Express.

Percy's driver turned on full steam and shouted for Percy to go back.

But Percy's wheels wouldn't turn quickly enough and Gordon couldn't stop.

Percy waited for the crash. The driver and fireman jumped out.

"Oo . . . ooh!" groaned Gordon. "Get out of my way!"

Percy opened his eyes. Gordon had stopped with Percy's buffers just a few inches from his own. But Percy had begun to move.

"I won't stay here. I'll run away!" he puffed.

He went straight through Edward's station and was so frightened that he ran right up Gordon's hill without stopping.

After that he was tired, but he couldn't stop.

Percy had no driver to shut off steam and put on his brakes.

"I shall have to run till my wheels wear out!" panted Percy. "Oh dear! Oh dear! I want to stop! I want to stop!" he puffed.

The man in the signal box saw that Percy was in trouble, so he kindly set the points.

Percy puffed wearily into a nice empty siding.

He was too tired now to care where he went.

"I – want – to – stop!
I – want – to – stop!" he puffed.

"I have stopped! I have stopped!" he said, thankfully.

"Sssh . . . Sssh!" he gasped as he ended up in a big bank of earth.

"Never mind, Percy," said the workmen as they dug him out. "You shall have a drink and some coal and then you'll feel better."

Gordon had arrived.

"Well done, Percy! You started so quickly that you stopped a nasty accident!"

"I'm sorry I was cheeky," said Percy. "You were clever to stop."

Then Gordon helped to pull Percy out from the bank.

Now Percy helps with the coaches in the yard. He is still cheeky because he is that sort of engine, but he is always *very* careful when he goes on the main line.

THOMAS

EDWARD

GORDON